# CAT'S GOT YOUR TONGUE?

## A Story for Children Afraid to Speak

## by Charles E. Schaefer, Ph.D.

### illustrated by Judith Friedman

**Magination Press** ● **New York**

My thanks to Rosemary McNiff
for her help on this book

Library of Congress Cataloging-in-Publication Data
Schaefer, Charles E.
    Cat's got your tongue?: a story for children afraid to
speak / by Charles E. Schaefer ; illustrated by Judith Friedman.
        p.  cm.
    Summary: Anna chooses not to talk when she enters kindergarten,
but then she discovers the pleasures of self-expression in the
security of a therapist's office.
    ISBN 0-945354-45-2 (cloth). — ISBN 0-945354-46-0 (paper)
    [1. Mutism, Elective—Fiction.   2. Kindergarten—Fiction.
3. Schools—Fiction.]  I. Friedman, Judith, 1945–  ill.
II. Title.
PZ7.S3316So   1992
[E]—dc20                                    91-42707
                                            CIP
                                            AC

Distributed in Canada by Book Center, 1140 Beaulac St., Montreal, Quebec H4R 1R8, Canada

Manufactured in the United States of America

10  9  8  7  6  5  4  3  2  1

# Introduction for Parents

At an early age, it is common for children to retreat to the safety of their parents when confronted by a stranger. Many parents have had to deal patiently with a young child who hangs onto them at family gatherings or who refuses to enter his or her preschool classroom. A number of kindergarteners and first graders become unusually quiet for the first week of school while they become familiar with a new teacher, new children, and a new setting. However, some children, in spite of their physical ability to speak, continue their silence for months and even years.

This book was created as a learning tool for children who suffer from short-term or long-term stranger anxiety, and for their families. Anna, who is diagnosed as an electively mute child, is the kindergartner in this story. She is treated sensitively and sympathetically; she is never punished or scolded because of her problem. Also, her behavior is never acceptingly referred to as "shy." Instead, the reader of and the listener to this story become happily aware of the positive aspects of speech, including self-expression and making new friends.

Not every child with stranger anxiety will refuse to speak outside the home and need the therapy that Anna did. But, hopefully, this book will make all these children feel that they are not alone.

Anna usually liked shopping with her mother, but not today. They found a pretty dress. Mama said it would be just right for the first day of school. The saleswoman put it in a bag and tried to hand it to Anna. But Anna just hurried from the store.

On the way home, they passed the school. Tomorrow Anna started kindergarten. She didn't want to go.

When they turned the corner, Anna saw her little brother, Lou,
playing ball with Grandma Garcia. "Come play, Anna," he called.
Lou didn't have to go to school. He could stay home with Mama.

The next morning, Anna didn't want to get dressed. She *slowly* put on her new dress and her stiff black shoes. At the kitchen table, she stared at her bowl of cereal. "Anna, eat up," said Mama. "You don't want to be late your first day of school."

With Lou in a stroller, Anna and Mama walked the one block to school. Anna dragged her heels all the way.

The school yard was filled with noisy children running, throwing balls, and playing hopscotch. Anna clung to her mother's hand. Then a loud bell rang. The children began lining up for class. Anna began to cry.

Her teacher, Ms. Spring, knelt down. "Say goodbye to your mother, Anna. Come on. I'll be your partner." Ms. Spring took Anna's hand and led the children into the classroom.

The children sat around long tables. They all gave their names, but Anna was too scared. She hid her face in her arms. Ms. Spring said, "OK, Anna, you can talk when you feel ready."

That evening, Anna's father asked her how she liked kindergarten. "OK," she said. She didn't want to tell him how scared she was. She hurried off to play with Lou.

A few days later, Mama said Anna would have to walk the one
block to school by herself. It was too cold for Lou to go outside.
That morning, Anna packed her stuffed kitten, Mittens, into
her school bag. After breakfast, they started to school together,
just as she had done with Mama.

Tucked into her coat, Mittens stayed with Anna at recess. Suddenly, Ronald ran over to get a runaway ball. "What do you have there?" he asked. Anna didn't answer.

"Cat's got your tongue! Cat's got your tongue!" he shouted as he grabbed Mittens and ran off. Anna ran after him. She grabbed him and hit him, trying to make him let go of Mittens.

When Ms. Spring separated the children, she asked what happened. Ronald blamed it all on Anna. "And what do you say, Anna?" asked Ms. Spring. But Anna just cried. Later that day, Ms. Spring gave Anna a note asking her parents to come to school.

The next day, when class let out, Anna's parents were waiting in the hall. Ms. Spring explained, "I am worried about Anna. She is not adjusting well to school. She has not spoken to me or to her classmates since school began." Ms. Spring said that the guidance counselor recommended they see a special doctor who could help Anna solve her problem.

The Garcia family visited the doctor's office that Friday. "Anna," said Dr. Linden, "I'd like to make it easier for you to talk to people when you want to." He smiled at her and her parents. "We can work together. Even Mittens can help." Anna didn't say a thing.

Anna visited Dr. Linden at his office every Friday after school. Dr. Linden read her stories. Then Anna drew pictures about the stories. Slowly, Anna began to talk about her pictures. Then about her family and herself.

Before long, Anna, Dr. Linden, and Mittens were putting on puppet shows. Their favorite was *Puss 'n' Boots.* "Anna, I bet your parents and teacher would love our puppet show. Would you like to show it to them?" Anna whispered, "Yes."

The next Friday after school, Dr. Linden, Anna, Mittens, and the rest of the puppet cast squeezed behind the classroom puppet theater. Anna peeked nervously through the curtain. Mama, Papa, and Ms. Spring looked funny sitting on the little chairs. Papa held his new video camera.

When the show was over, Mama, Papa, and Ms. Spring clapped loudly. They told Anna how proud they were of her. Dr. Linden said she was a star. He pinned a gold star on Anna's collar. "Thank you," she said.

The following week, Dr. Linden visited Anna and Ms. Spring in their classroom after school. They talked about the puppet show while they played checkers. Ms. Spring asked Anna if she wanted to show the videotape to the class. Anna smiled and said, "Yes."

On Monday, Ms. Spring played the tape for the class. Everyone clapped. Anna felt proud and happy.

Her classmate, Laurinda, rang her doorbell that afternoon. She was holding a box with holes in the side. "My cat had kittens," she said. "When I saw your puppet show today, I thought you might like to have a real puss 'n' boots. Your mom told mine it was OK." Anna and her new friend had fun playing with the little black and white kitten.

After that day, Anna began speaking more in class and making new friends. Now, when something new or strange scares her, she remembers her puppet show and how good she felt. Anna feels brave enough to speak even when she is afraid.

# Magination Press Books

**Into the Great Forest:** A Story for Children Away from Parents for the First Time

**Russell Is Extra Special:** A Book About Autism for Children

**Cat's Got Your Tongue?** A Story for Children Afraid to Speak

**More Annie Stories:** Therapeutic Storytelling Techniques

**Julia, Mungo, and the Earthquake:** A Story for Young People About Epilepsy

**Tell Me A Story, Paint Me the Sun:** When a Girl Feels Ignored by Her Father

**Night Light:** A Story for Children Afraid of the Dark

**Putting on the Brakes:** Young People's Guide to Understanding Attention Deficit Hyperactivity Disorder (ADHD)

**The Potty Chronicles:** A Story to Help Children Adjust to Toilet Training

**Tanya and the Tobo Man:** A Story in English and Spanish for Children Entering Therapy

**Wish Upon A Star:** A Story for Children with a Parent Who Is Mentally Ill

**Gran-Gran's Best Trick:** A Story for Children Who Have Lost Someone They Love

**Scary Night Visitors:** A Story for Children with Bedtime Fears

**Ignatius Finds Help**: A Story About Psychotherapy for Children

**Jessica and the Wolf:** A Story for Children Who Have Bad Dreams

**The Blammo-Surprise! Book:** A Story to Help Children Overcome Fears

**Zachary's New Home:** A Story for Foster and Adopted Children

**Clouds and Clocks:** A Story for Children Who Soil

**Sammy the Elephant and Mr. Camel:** A Story to Help Children Overcome Bedwetting

**Otto Learns About His Medicine:** A Story About Medication for Hyperactive Children

**Double-Dip Feelings:** Stories to Help Children Understand Emotions

**This is Me and My Single Parent**: A Workbook for Children and Single Parents

**This is Me and My Two Families**: A Workbook for Children in Stepfamilies

**Cartoon Magic:** How to Help Children Discover Their Rainbows Within

**Robby Really Transforms**: A Story About Grown-Ups Helping Children

**Lizard Tales**: Observations About Life